Watchbird

Books by Robert Sheckley:

Watchbird

Robert Sheckley

ÆGYPAN PRESS

This story first in the February, 1953, issue of *Galaxy Science Fiction.*

Special thanks to Greg Weeks, Stephen Blundell, and the On-line Distributed Proofreading Team at http://www.pgdp.net.

Watchbird
A publication of
ÆGYPAN PRESS

www.aegypan.com

Strange how often the Millennium has been at hand. The idea is peace on Earth, see, and the way to do it is by figuring out angles.

*W*hen Gelsen entered, he saw that the rest of the watchbird manufacturers were already present. There were six of them, not counting himself, and the room was blue with expensive cigar smoke.

"Hi, Charlie," one of them called as he came in.

The rest broke off conversation long enough to wave a casual greeting at him. As a watchbird manufacturer, he was a member manufacturer of salvation, he reminded himself wryly. Very exclusive. You must have a certified government contract if you want to save the human race.

"The government representative isn't here yet," one of the men told him. "He's due any minute."

"We're getting the green light," another said.

"Fine." Gelsen found a chair near the door and looked around the room. It was like a convention, or a Boy Scout rally. The six men made up for their lack of numbers by sheer volume. The president of Southern Consolidated was talking at the top of his lungs about watchbird's enormous durability. The two presidents he was talking at were grinning, nodding, one trying to interrupt with the results of a test he had run on watchbird's resourcefulness, the other talking about the new recharging apparatus.

The other three men were in their own little group, delivering what sounded like a panegyric to watchbird.

Gelsen noticed that all of them stood straight and tall, like the saviors they felt they were. He didn't find it funny. Up to a few days ago he had felt that way himself. He had considered himself a pot-bellied, slightly balding saint.

*H*e sighed and lighted a cigarette. At the beginning of the project, he had been as enthusiastic as the others. He remembered saying to Macintyre, his chief engineer, "Mac, a new day is coming. Watchbird is the Answer." And Macintyre had nodded very profoundly – another watchbird convert.

How wonderful it had seemed then! A simple, reliable answer to one of mankind's greatest problems, all wrapped and packaged in a pound of incorruptible metal, crystal and plastics.

Perhaps that was the very reason he was doubting it now. Gelsen suspected that you don't solve human problems so easily. There had to be a catch somewhere.

After all, murder was an old problem, and watchbird too new a solution.

"Gentlemen —" They had been talking so heatedly that they hadn't noticed the government representative entering. Now the room became quiet at once.

"Gentlemen," the plump government man said, "the President, with the consent of Congress, has acted to form a watchbird division for every city and town in the country."

The men burst into a spontaneous shout of triumph. They were going to have their chance to save the world after all, Gelsen thought, and worriedly asked himself what was wrong with that.

He listened carefully as the government man outlined the distribution scheme. The country was to be divided into seven areas, each to be supplied and serviced by one manufacturer. This meant monopoly, of course, but a necessary one. Like the telephone service, it was in the public's best interests. You couldn't have competition in watchbird service. Watchbird was for everyone.

"The President hopes," the representative continued, "that full watchbird service will be installed in the shortest possible time. You will have top priorities on strategic metals, manpower, and so forth."

"Speaking for myself," the president of Southern Consolidated said, "I expect to have the first batch of watchbirds distributed within the week. Production is all set up."

*T*he rest of the men were equally ready. The factories had been prepared to roll out the watchbirds for months now. The final standardized equipment had been agreed upon, and only the Presidential go-ahead had been lacking.

"Fine," the representative said. "If that is all, I think we can — is there a question?"

"Yes, sir," Gelsen said. "I want to know if the present model is the one we are going to manufacture."

"Of course," the representative said. "It's the most advanced."

"I have an objection." Gelsen stood up. His colleagues were glaring coldly at him. Obviously he was delaying the advent of the golden age.

"What is your objection?" the representative asked.

"First, let me say that I am one hundred percent in favor of a machine to stop murder. It's been needed for a long time. I object only to the watchbird's learning circuits. They serve, in effect, to animate the machine and give it a pseudo-consciousness. I can't approve of that."

"But, Mr. Gelsen, you yourself testified that the watchbird would not be completely efficient unless such circuits were introduced. Without them, the watchbirds could stop only an estimated seventy percent of murders."

"I know that," Gelsen said, feeling extremely uncomfortable. "I believe there might be a moral danger in allowing a machine to make decisions that are rightfully Man's," he declared doggedly.

"Oh, come now, Gelsen," one of the corporation presidents said. "It's nothing of the sort. The watchbird will only reinforce the decisions made by honest men from the beginning of time."

"I think that is true," the representative agreed. "But I can understand how Mr. Gelsen feels. It is sad that we must put a human problem into the hands of a machine, sadder still that we must have a machine enforce our laws. But I ask you to remember, Mr. Gelsen, that there is no other possible way of stopping a murderer *before he strikes*. It would be unfair to the many innocent people killed every year if we were to restrict watchbird on philosophical grounds. Don't you agree that I'm right?"

"Yes, I suppose I do," Gelsen said unhappily. He had told himself all that a thousand times, but something still bothered him. Perhaps he would talk it over with Macintyre.

As the conference broke up, a thought struck him. He grinned.

A lot of policemen were going to be out of work!

"Now what do you think of that?" Officer Celtrics demanded. "Fifteen years in Homicide and a machine is replacing me." He wiped a large red hand across his forehead and leaned against the captain's desk. "Ain't science marvelous?"

Two other policemen, late of Homicide, nodded glumly.

"Don't worry about it," the captain said. "We'll find a home for you in Larceny, Celtrics. You'll like it here."

"I just can't get over it," Celtrics complained. "A lousy little piece of tin and glass is going to solve all the crimes."

"Not quite," the captain said. "The watchbirds are supposed to prevent the crimes before they happen."

"Then how'll they be crimes?" one of the policeman asked. "I mean they can't hang you for murder until you commit one, can they?"

"That's not the idea," the captain said. "The watchbirds are supposed to stop a man before he commits a murder."

"Then no one arrests him?" Celtrics asked.

"I don't know how they're going to work that out," the captain admitted.

The men were silent for a while. The captain yawned and examined his watch.

"The thing I don't understand," Celtrics said, still leaning on the captain's desk, "is just how do they do it? How did it start, Captain?"

The captain studied Celtrics' face for possible irony; after all, watchbird had been in the papers for months. But then he remembered that Celtrics, like his side-kicks, rarely bothered to turn past the sports pages.

"Well," the captain said, trying to remember what he had read in the Sunday supplements, "these scientists were working on criminology. They were studying murderers, to find out what made them tick. So they found that murderers throw out a different sort of brain wave from ordinary people. And their glands act funny, too. All this happens when they're about to commit a murder. So these scientists worked out a special machine to flash red or something when these brain waves turned on."

"Scientists," Celtrics said bitterly.

"Well, after the scientists had this machine, they didn't know what to do with it. It was too big to move around, and murderers didn't drop in often enough to make it flash. So they built it into a smaller unit and tried it out in a few police stations. I think they tried one upstate. But it didn't work so good. You couldn't get to the crime in time. That's why they built the watchbirds."

"I don't think they'll stop no criminals," one of the policemen insisted.

"They sure will. I read the test results. They can smell him out before he commits a crime. And when they reach him, they give him a powerful shock or something. It'll stop him."

"You closing up Homicide, Captain?" Celtrics asked.

"Nope," the captain said. "I'm leaving a skeleton crew in until we see how these birds do."

"Hah," Celtrics said. "Skeleton crew. That's funny."

"Sure," the captain said. "Anyhow, I'm going to leave some men on. It seems the birds don't stop all murders."

"Why not?"

"Some murderers don't have these brain waves," the captain answered, trying to remember what the newspaper article had said. "Or their glands don't work or something."

"Which ones don't they stop?" Celtrics asked, with professional curiosity.

"I don't know. But I hear they got the damned things fixed so they're going to stop all of them soon."

"How they working that?"

"They learn. The watchbirds, I mean. Just like people."

"You kidding me?"

"Nope."

"Well," Celtrics said, "I think I'll just keep old Betsy oiled, just in case. You can't trust these scientists."

"Right."

"Birds!" Celtrics scoffed.

Over the town, the watchbird soared in a long, lazy curve. Its aluminum hide glistened in the morning sun, and dots of light danced on its stiff wings. Silently it flew.

Silently, but with all senses functioning. Built-in kinesthetics told the watchbird where it was, and held it in a long search curve. Its eyes and ears operated as one unit, searching, seeking.

And then something happened! The watchbird's electronically fast reflexes picked up the edge of a sensation. A correlation center tested it, matching it with electrical and chemical data in its memory files. A relay tripped.

Down the watchbird spiraled, coming in on the increasingly strong sensation. It *smelled* the outpouring of certain glands, *tasted* a deviant brain wave.

Fully alerted and armed, it spun and banked in the bright morning sunlight.

Dinelli was so intent he didn't see the watchbird coming. He had his gun poised, and his eyes pleaded with the big grocer.

"Don't come no closer."

"You lousy little punk," the grocer said, and took another step forward. "Rob me? I'll break every bone in your puny body."

The grocer, too stupid or too courageous to understand the threat of the gun, advanced on the little thief.

"All right," Dinelli said, in a thorough state of panic. "All right, sucker, take —"

A bolt of electricity knocked him on his back. The gun went off, smashing a breakfast food display.

"What in hell?" the grocer asked, staring at the stunned thief. And then he saw a flash of silver wings. "Well, I'm really damned. Those watchbirds work!"

He stared until, the wings disappeared in the sky. Then he telephoned the police.

The watchbird returned to his search curve. His thinking center correlated the new facts he had learned about murder. Several of these he hadn't known before.

This new information was simultaneously flashed to all the other watchbirds and their information was flashed back to him.

New information, methods, definitions were constantly passing between them.

*N*ow that the watchbirds were rolling off the assembly line in a steady stream, Gelsen allowed himself to relax. A loud contented hum filled his plant. Orders were being filled on time, with top priorities given to the biggest cities in his area, and working down to the smallest towns.

"All smooth, Chief," Macintyre said, coming in the door. He had just completed a routine inspection.

"Fine. Have a seat."

The big engineer sat down and lighted a cigarette.

"We've been working on this for some time," Gelsen said, when he couldn't think of anything else.

"We sure have," Macintyre agreed. He leaned back and inhaled deeply. He had been one of the consulting engineers on the original watchbird. That was six years back. He had been working for Gelsen ever since, and the men had become good friends.

"The thing I wanted to ask you was this —" Gelsen paused. He couldn't think how to phrase what he wanted. Instead he asked, "What do you think of the watchbirds, Mac?"

"Who, me?" The engineer grinned nervously. He had been eating, drinking and sleeping watchbird ever since its inception. He had never found it necessary to have an attitude. "Why, I think it's great."

"I don't mean that," Gelsen said. He realized that what he wanted was to have someone understand his point of view. "I mean do you figure there might be some danger in machine thinking?"

"I don't think so, Chief. Why do you ask?"

"Look, I'm no scientist or engineer. I've just handled cost and production and let you boys worry about how. But as a layman, watchbird is starting to frighten me."

"No reason for that."

"I don't like the idea of the learning circuits."

"But why not?" Then Macintyre grinned again. "I know. You're like a lot of people, Chief — afraid your machines are going to wake up and say, 'What are we doing here? Let's go out and rule the world.' Is that it?"

"Maybe something like that," Gelsen admitted.

"No chance of it," Macintyre said. "The watchbirds are complex, I'll admit, but an M.I.T. calculator is a

whole lot more complex. And it hasn't got consciousness."

"No. But the watchbirds can *learn.*"

"Sure. So can all the new calculators. Do you think
they'll team up with the watchbirds?"

Gelsen felt annoyed at Macintyre, and even more
annoyed at himself for being ridiculous. "It's a fact
that the watchbirds can put their learning into action.
No one is monitoring them."

"So that's the trouble," Macintyre said.

"I've been thinking of getting out of watchbird."
Gelsen hadn't realized it until that moment.

"Look, Chief," Macintyre said. "Will you take an
engineer's word on this?"

"Let's hear it."

"The watchbirds are no more dangerous than an
automobile, an IBM calculator or a thermometer. They
have no more consciousness or volition than those
things. The watchbirds are built to respond to certain
stimuli, and to carry out certain operations when they
receive that stimuli."

"And the learning circuits?"

"You have to have those," Macintyre said patiently,
as though explaining the whole thing to a ten-year-old.
"The purpose of the watchbird is to frustrate all mur-
der-attempts, right? Well, only certain murderers give
out these stimuli. In order to stop all of them, the
watchbird has to search out new definitions of murder
and correlate them with what it already knows."

"I think it's inhuman," Gelsen said.

"That's the best thing about it. The watchbirds are
unemotional. Their reasoning is non-anthropomor-

phic. You can't bribe them or drug them. You shouldn't fear them, either."

The intercom on Gelsen's desk buzzed. He ignored it.

"I know all this," Gelsen said. "But, still, sometimes I feel like the man who invented dynamite. He thought it would only be used for blowing up tree stumps."

"You didn't invent watchbird."

"I still feel morally responsible because I manufacture them."

The intercom buzzed again, and Gelsen irritably punched a button.

"The reports are in on the first week of watchbird operation," his secretary told him.

"How do they look?"

"Wonderful, sir."

"Send them in in fifteen minutes." Gelsen switched the intercom off and turned back to Macintyre, who was cleaning his fingernails with a wooden match. "Don't you think that this represents a trend in human thinking? The mechanical god? The electronic father?"

"Chief," Macintyre said, "I think you should study watchbird more closely. Do you know what's built into the circuits?"

"Only generally."

"First, there is a purpose. Which is to stop living organisms from committing murder. Two, murder may be defined as an act of violence, consisting of breaking, mangling, maltreating or otherwise stopping the functions of a living organism by a living organism. Three, most murderers are detectable by certain chemical and electrical changes."

Macintyre paused to light another cigarette. "Those conditions take care of the routine functions. Then, for the learning circuits, there are two more conditions. Four, there are some living organisms who commit murder without the signs mentioned in three. Five, these can be detected by data applicable to condition two."

"I see," Gelsen said.

"You realize how foolproof it is?"

"I suppose so." Gelsen hesitated a moment. "I guess that's all."

"Right," the engineer said, and left.

Gelsen thought for a few moments. There *couldn't* be anything wrong with the watchbirds.

"Send in the reports," he said into the intercom.

*H*igh above the lighted buildings of the city, the watchbird soared. It was dark, but in the distance the watchbird could see another, and another beyond that. For this was a large city.

To prevent murder . . .

There was more to watch for now. New information had crossed the invisible network that connected all watchbirds. New data, new ways of detecting the violence of murder.

There! The edge of a sensation! Two watchbirds dipped simultaneously. One had received the scent a fraction of a second before the other. He continued down while the other resumed monitoring.

Condition four, there are some living organisms who commit murder without the signs mentioned in condition three.

Through his new information, the watchbird knew by extrapolation that this organism was bent on murder, even though the characteristic chemical and electrical smells were absent.

The watchbird, all senses acute, closed in on the organism. He found what he wanted, and dived.

Roger Greco leaned against a building, his hands in his pockets. In his left hand was the cool butt of a .45. Greco waited patiently.

He wasn't thinking of anything in particular, just relaxing against a building, waiting for a man. Greco didn't know why the man was to be killed. He didn't care. Greco's lack of curiosity was part of his value. The other part was his skill.

One bullet, neatly placed in the head of a man he didn't know. It didn't excite him or sicken him. It was a job, just like anything else. You killed a man. So?

As Greco's victim stepped out of a building, Greco lifted the .45 out of his pocket. He released the safety and braced the gun with his right hand. He still wasn't thinking of anything as he took aim . . .

And was knocked off his feet.

Greco thought he had been shot. He struggled up again, looked around, and sighted foggily on his victim.

Again he was knocked down.

This time he lay on the ground, trying to draw a bead. He never thought of stopping, for Greco was a craftsman.

With the next blow, everything went black. Permanently, because the watchbird's duty was to protect the object of violence — *at whatever cost to the murderer.*

The victim walked to his car. He hadn't noticed anything unusual. Everything had happened in silence.

Gelsen was feeling pretty good. The watchbirds had been operating perfectly. Crimes of violence had been cut in half, and cut again. Dark alleys were no longer mouths of horror. Parks and playgrounds were not places to shun after dusk.

Of course, there were still robberies. Petty thievery flourished, and embezzlement, larceny, forgery and a hundred other crimes.

But that wasn't so important. You could regain lost money — never a lost life.

Gelsen was ready to admit that he had been wrong about the watchbirds. They *were* doing a job that humans had been unable to accomplish.

The first hint of something wrong came that morning.

Macintyre came into his office. He stood silently in front of Gelsen's desk, looking annoyed and a little embarrassed.

"What's the matter, Mac?" Gelsen asked.

"One of the watchbirds went to work on a slaughterhouse man. Knocked him out."

Gelsen thought about it for a moment. Yes, the watchbirds would do that. With their new learning circuits, they had probably defined the killing of animals as murder.

"Tell the packers to mechanize their slaughtering," Gelsen said. "I never liked that business myself."

"All right," Macintyre said. He pursed his lips, then shrugged his shoulders and left.

Gelsen stood beside his desk, thinking. Couldn't the watchbirds differentiate between a murderer and a man engaged in a legitimate profession? No, evidently not. To them, murder was murder. No exceptions. He frowned. That might take a little ironing out in the circuits.

But not too much, he decided hastily. Just make them a little more discriminating.

He sat down again and buried himself in paperwork, trying to avoid the edge of an old fear.

*T*hey strapped the prisoner into the chair and fitted the electrode to his leg.

"Oh, oh," he moaned, only half-conscious now of what they were doing.

They fitted the helmet over his shaved head and tightened the last straps. He continued to moan softly.

And then the watchbird swept in. How he had come, no one knew. Prisons are large and strong, with many locked doors, but the watchbird was there —

To stop a murder.

"Get that thing out of here!" the warden shouted, and reached for the switch. The watchbird knocked him down.

"Stop that!" a guard screamed, and grabbed for the switch himself. He was knocked to the floor beside the warden.

"This isn't murder, you idiot!" another guard said. He drew his gun to shoot down the glittering, wheeling metal bird.

Anticipating, the watchbird smashed him back against the wall.

There was silence in the room. After a while, the man in the helmet started to giggle. Then he stopped.

The watchbird stood on guard, fluttering in mid-air —

Making sure no murder was done.

New data flashed along the watchbird network. Un-monitored, independent, the thousands of watchbirds received and acted upon it.

The breaking, mangling or otherwise stopping the functions of a living organism by a living organism. New acts to stop.

"Damn you, git going!" Farmer Ollister shouted, and raised his whip again. The horse balked, and the wagon rattled and shook as he edged sideways.

"You lousy hunk of pigmeal, git going!" the farmer yelled and he raised the whip again.

It never fell. An alert watchbird, sensing violence, had knocked him out of his seat.

A living organism? What is a living organism? The watchbirds extended their definitions as they became aware of more facts. And, of course, this gave them more work.

The deer was just visible at the edge of the woods. The hunter raised his rifle, and took careful aim.

He didn't have time to shoot.

*W*ith his free hand, Gelsen mopped perspiration from his face. "All right," he said into the telephone. He listened to the stream of vituperation from the other end, then placed the receiver gently in its cradle.

"What was that one?" Macintyre asked. He was unshaven, tie loose, shirt unbuttoned.

"Another fisherman," Gelsen said. "It seems the watchbirds won't let him fish even though his family is starving. What are we going to do about it, he wants to know."

"How many hundred is that?"

"I don't know. I haven't opened the mail."

"Well, I figured out where the trouble is," Macintyre said gloomily, with the air of a man who knows just how he blew up the Earth — after it was too late.

"Let's hear it."

"Everybody took it for granted that we wanted all murder stopped. We figured the watchbirds would think as we do. We ought to have qualified the conditions."

"I've got an idea," Gelsen said, "that we'd have to know just why and what murder is, before we could qualify the conditions properly. And if we knew that, we wouldn't need the watchbirds."

"Oh, I don't know about that. They just have to be told that some things which look like murder are not murder."

"But why should they stop fisherman?" Gelsen asked.

"Why shouldn't they? Fish and animals are living organisms. We just don't think that killing them is murder."

The telephone rang. Gelsen glared at it and punched the intercom. "I told you no more calls, no matter what."

"This is from Washington," his secretary said. "I thought you'd —"

"Sorry." Gelsen picked up the telephone. "Yes. Certainly is a mess . . . Have they? All right, I certainly will." He put down the telephone.

"Short and sweet," he told Macintyre. "We're to shut down temporarily."

"That won't be so easy," Macintyre said. "The watchbirds operate independent of any central control, you know. They come back once a week for a repair checkup. We'll have to turn them off then, one by one."

"Well, let's get to it. Monroe over on the Coast has shut down about a quarter of his birds."

"I think I can dope out a restricting circuit," Macintyre said.

"Fine," Gelsen replied bitterly. "You make me very happy."

*T*he watchbirds were learning rapidly, expanding and adding to their knowledge. Loosely defined abstractions were extended, acted upon and re-extended.

To stop murder . . .

Metal and electrons reason well, but not in a human fashion.

A living organism? *Any* living organism!

The watchbirds set themselves the task of protecting all living things.

The fly buzzed around the room, lighting on a tabletop, pausing a moment, then darting to a window-sill.

The old man stalked it, a rolled newspaper in his hand.

Murderer!

The watchbirds swept down and saved the fly in the nick of time.

The old man writhed on the floor a minute and then was silent. He had been given only a mild shock, but it had been enough for his fluttery, cranky heart.

His victim had been saved, though, and this was the important thing. Save the victim and give the aggressor his just desserts.

Gelsen demanded angrily, "Why aren't they being turned off?"

The assistant control engineer gestured. In a corner of the repair room lay the senior control engineer. He was just regaining consciousness.

"He tried to turn one of them off," the assistant engineer said. Both his hands were knotted together. He was making a visible effort not to shake.

"That's ridiculous. They haven't got any sense of self-preservation."

"Then turn them off yourself. Besides, I don't think any more are going to come."

What could have happened? Gelsen began to piece it together. The watchbirds still hadn't decided on the limits of a living organism. When some of them were turned off in the Monroe plant, the rest must have correlated the data.

So they had been forced to assume that they were living organisms, as well.

No one had ever told them otherwise. Certainly they carried on most of the functions of living organisms.

Then the old fears hit him. Gelsen trembled and hurried out of the repair room. He wanted to find Macintyre in a hurry.

*T*he nurse handed the surgeon the sponge.

"Scalpel."

She placed it in his hand. He started to make the first incision. And then he was aware of a disturbance.

"Who let that thing in?"

"I don't know," the nurse said, her voice muffled by the mask.

"Get it out of here."

The nurse waved her arms at the bright winged thing, but it fluttered over her head.

The surgeon proceeded with the incision — as long as he was able.

The watchbird drove him away and stood guard.

"Telephone the watchbird company!" the surgeon ordered. "Get them to turn the thing off."

The watchbird was preventing violence to a living organism.

The surgeon stood by helplessly while his patient died.

*F*luttering high above the network of highways, the watchbird watched and waited. It had been constantly working for weeks now, without rest or repair. Rest and repair were impossible, because the watchbird couldn't allow itself — a living organism — to be murdered. And that was what happened when watchbirds returned to the factory.

There was a built-in order to return, after the lapse of a certain time period. But the watchbird had a stronger order to obey — preservation of life, including its own.

The definitions of murder were almost infinitely extended now, impossible to cope with. But the watchbird didn't consider that. It responded to its stimuli, whenever they came and whatever their source.

There was a new definition of living organism in its memory files. It had come as a result of the watchbird discovery that watchbirds were living organisms. And it had enormous ramifications.

The stimuli came! For the hundredth time that day, the bird wheeled and banked, dropping swiftly down to stop murder.

Jackson yawned and pulled his car to a shoulder of the road. He didn't notice the glittering dot in the sky. There was no reason for him to. Jackson wasn't contemplating murder, by any human definition.

This was a good spot for a nap, he decided. He had been driving for seven straight hours and his eyes were starting to fog. He reached out to turn off the ignition key —

And was knocked back against the side of the car.

"What in hell's wrong with you?" he asked indignantly. "All I want to do is —" He reached for the key again, and again he was smacked back.

Jackson knew better than to try a third time. He had been listening to the radio and he knew what the watchbirds did to stubborn violators.

"You mechanical jerk," he said to the waiting metal bird. "A car's not alive. I'm not trying to kill it."

But the watchbird only knew that a certain operation resulted in stopping an organism. The car was certainly a functioning organism. Wasn't it of metal, as were the watchbirds? Didn't it run?

Macintyre said, "Without repairs they'll run down." He shoved a pile of specification sheets out of his way.

"How soon?" Gelsen asked.

"Six months to a year. Say a year, barring accidents."

"A year," Gelsen said. "In the meantime, everything is stopping dead. Do you know the latest?"

"What?"

"The watchbirds have decided that the Earth is a living organism. They won't allow farmers to break ground for plowing. And, of course, everything else is a living organism — rabbits, beetles, flies, wolves, mosquitoes, lions, crocodiles, crows, and smaller forms of life such as bacteria."

"I know," Macintyre said.

"And you tell me they'll wear out in six months or a year. What happens *now?* What are we going to eat in six months?"

The engineer rubbed his chin. "We'll have to do something quick and fast. Ecological balance is gone to hell."

"Fast isn't the word. Instantaneously would be better." Gelsen lighted his thirty-fifth cigarette for the day. "At least I have the bitter satisfaction of saying, 'I told you so.' Although I'm just as responsible as the rest of the machine-worshipping fools."

Macintyre wasn't listening. He was thinking about watchbirds. "Like the rabbit plague in Australia."

"The death rate is mounting," Gelsen said. "Famine. Floods. Can't cut down trees. Doctors can't — what was that you said about Australia?"

"The rabbits," Macintyre repeated. "Hardly any left in Australia now."

"Why? How was it done?"

"Oh, found some kind of germ that attacked only rabbits. I think it was propagated by mosquitos —"

"Work on that," Gelsen said. "You might have something. I want you to get on the telephone, ask for an emergency hookup with the engineers of the other companies. Hurry it up. Together you may be able to dope out something."

"Right," Macintyre said. He grabbed a handful of blank paper and hurried to the telephone.

"What did I tell you?" Officer Celtrics said. He grinned at the captain. "Didn't I tell you scientists were nuts?"

"I didn't say you were wrong, did I?" the captain asked.

"No, but you weren't *sure.*"

"Well, I'm sure now. You'd better get going. There's plenty of work for you."

"I know." Celtrics drew his revolver from its holster, checked it and put it back. "Are all the boys back, Captain?"

"All?" the captain laughed humorlessly. "Homicide has increased by fifty percent. There's more murder now than there's ever been."

"Sure," Celtrics said. "The watchbirds are too busy guarding cars and slugging spiders." He started toward the door, then turned for a parting shot.

"Take my word, Captain. Machines are *stupid.*"

The captain nodded.

*T*housands of watchbirds, trying to stop countless millions of murders — a hopeless task. But the watchbirds didn't hope. Without consciousness, they experienced no sense of accomplishment, no fear of failure. Patiently they went about their jobs, obeying each stimulus as it came.

They couldn't be everywhere at the same time, but it wasn't necessary to be. People learned quickly what the watchbirds didn't like and refrained from doing it. It just wasn't safe. With their high speed and superfast senses, the watchbirds got around quickly.

And now they meant business. In their original directives there had been a provision made for killing a murderer, if all other means failed.

Why spare a murderer?

It backfired. The watchbirds extracted the fact that murder and crimes of violence had increased geometrically since they had begun operation. This was true, because their new definitions increased the possibilities of murder. But to the watchbirds, the rise showed that the first methods had failed.

Simple logic. If A doesn't work, try B. The watchbirds shocked to kill.

Slaughterhouses in Chicago stopped and cattle starved to death in their pens, because farmers in the Midwest couldn't cut hay or harvest grain.

No one had told the watchbirds that all life depends on carefully balanced murders.

Starvation didn't concern the watchbirds, since it was an act of omission.

Their interest lay only in acts of commission.

Hunters sat home, glaring at the silver dots in the sky, longing to shoot them down. But for the most part, they didn't try. The watchbirds were quick to sense the murder intent and to punish it.

Fishing boats swung idle at their moorings in San Pedro and Gloucester. Fish were living organisms.

Farmers cursed and spat and died, trying to harvest the crop. Grain was alive and thus worthy of protection. Potatoes were as important to the watchbird as any other living organism. The death of a blade of grass was equal to the assassination of a President —

To the watchbirds.

And, of course, certain machines were living. This followed, since the watchbirds were machines and living.

God help you if you maltreated your radio. Turning it off meant killing it. Obviously — its voice was silenced, the red glow of its tubes faded, it grew cold.

The watchbirds tried to guard their other charges. Wolves were slaughtered, trying to kill rabbits. Rabbits were electrocuted, trying to eat vegetables. Creepers were burned out in the act of strangling trees.

A butterfly was executed, caught in the act of outraging a rose.

This control was spasmodic, because of the fewness of the watchbirds. A billion watchbirds couldn't have carried out the ambitious project set by the thousands.

The effect was of a murderous force, ten thousand bolts of irrational lightning raging around the country, striking a thousand times a day.

Lightning which anticipated your moves and punished your intentions.

"Gentlemen, *please,*" the government representative begged. "We must hurry."

The seven manufacturers stopped talking.

"Before we begin this meeting formally," the president of Monroe said, "I want to say something. We do not feel ourselves responsible for this unhappy state of affairs. It was a government project; the government must accept the responsibility, both moral and financial."

Gelsen shrugged his shoulders. It was hard to believe that these men, just a few weeks ago, had been willing to accept the glory of saving the world. Now they wanted to shrug off the responsibility when the salvation went amiss.

"I'm positive that that need not concern us now," the representative assured him. "We must hurry. You engineers have done an excellent job. I am proud of the cooperation you have shown in this emergency. You are hereby empowered to put the outlined plan into action."

"Wait a minute," Gelsen said.

"There is no time."

"The plan's no good."

"Don't you think it will work?"

"Of course it will work. But I'm afraid the cure will be worse than the disease."

The manufacturers looked as though they would have enjoyed throttling Gelsen. He didn't hesitate.

"Haven't we learned yet?" he asked. "Don't you see that you can't cure human problems by mechanization?"

"Mr. Gelsen," the president of Monroe said, "I would enjoy hearing you philosophize, but, unfortunately, people are being killed. Crops are being ruined. There is famine in some sections of the country already. The watchbirds must be stopped at once!"

"Murder must be stopped, too. I remember all of us agreeing upon that. But this is not the way!"

"What would you suggest?" the representative asked.

Gelsen took a deep breath. What he was about to say took all the courage he had.

"Let the watchbirds run down by themselves," Gelsen suggested.

There was a near-riot. The government representative broke it up.

"Let's take our lesson," Gelsen urged, "admit that we were wrong trying to cure human problems by mechanical means. Start again. Use machines, yes, but not as judges and teachers and fathers."

"Ridiculous," the representative said coldly. "Mr. Gelsen, you are overwrought. I suggest you control yourself." He cleared his throat. "All of you are ordered by the President to carry out the plan you have submitted." He looked sharply at Gelsen. "Not to do so will be treason."

"I'll cooperate to the best of my ability," Gelsen said.

"Good. Those assembly lines must be rolling within the week."

Gelsen walked out of the room alone. Now he was confused again. Had he been right or was he just another visionary? Certainly, he hadn't explained himself with much clarity.

Did he know what he meant?

Gelsen cursed under his breath. He wondered why he couldn't ever be sure of anything. Weren't there any values he could hold on to?

He hurried to the airport and to his plant.

*T*he watchbird was operating erratically now. Many of its delicate parts were out of line, worn by almost continuous operation. But gallantly it responded when the stimuli came.

A spider was attacking a fly. The watchbird swooped down to the rescue.

Simultaneously, it became aware of something overhead. The watchbird wheeled to meet it.

There was a sharp crackle and a power bolt whizzed by the watchbird's wing. Angrily, it spat a shock wave.

The attacker was heavily insulated. Again it spat at the watchbird. This time, a bolt smashed through a wing, the watchbird darted away, but the attacker went after it in a burst of speed, throwing out more crackling power.

The watchbird fell, but managed to send out its message. Urgent! A new menace to living organisms and this was the deadliest yet!

Other watchbirds around the country integrated the message. Their thinking centers searched for an answer.

*W*ell, Chief, they bagged fifty today," Macintyre said, coming into Gelsen's office.

"Fine," Gelsen said, not looking at the engineer.

"Not so fine." Macintyre sat down. "Lord, I'm tired! It was seventy-two yesterday."

"I know." On Gelsen's desk were several dozen lawsuits, which he was sending to the government with a prayer.

"They'll pick up again, though," Macintyre said confidently. "The Hawks are especially built to hunt down watchbirds. They're stronger, faster, and they've got better armor. We really rolled them out in a hurry, huh?"

"We sure did."

"The watchbirds are pretty good, too," Macintyre had to admit. "They're learning to take cover. They're trying a lot of stunts. You know, each one that goes down tells the others something."

Gelsen didn't answer.

"But anything the watchbirds can do, the Hawks can do better," Macintyre said cheerfully. "The Hawks have special learning circuits for hunting. They're more flexible than the watchbirds. They learn faster."

Gelsen gloomily stood up, stretched, and walked to the window. The sky was blank. Looking out, he realized that his uncertainties were over. Right or wrong, he had made up his mind.

"Tell me," he said, still watching the sky, "what will the Hawks hunt after they get all the watchbirds?"

"Huh?" Macintyre said. "Why —"

"Just to be on the safe side, you'd better design something to hunt down the Hawks. Just in case, I mean."

"You think —"

"All I know is that the Hawks are self-controlled. So were the watchbirds. Remote control would have been too slow, the argument went on. The idea was to get the watchbirds and get them fast. That meant no restricting circuits."

"We can dope something out," Macintyre said uncertainly.

"You've got an aggressive machine up in the air now. A murder machine. Before that it was an anti-murder machine. Your next gadget will have to be even more self-sufficient, won't it?"

Macintyre didn't answer.

"I don't hold you responsible," Gelsen said. "It's me. It's everyone."

In the air outside was a swift-moving dot.

"That's what comes," said Gelsen, "of giving a machine the job that was our own responsibility."

*O*verhead, a Hawk was zeroing in on a watchbird.

The armored murder machine had learned a lot in a few days. Its sole function was to kill. At present it was impelled toward a certain type of living organism, metallic like itself.

But the Hawk had just discovered that there were other types of living organisms, too —

Which had to be murdered.

— Robert Sheckley